PARENTS' MAGAZINE PRESS
NEW YORK

# SCUTTLE
## THE STOWAWAY MOUSE

### BY JEAN AND NANCY SOULE
### PICTURES BY BARBARA REMINGTON

for
RICHARD JOSEPH,
the newest member
of our family,
in the hope that he
will someday enjoy
this book.

Down by the sea where the great ships sail
Lived Scuttle, a mouse with a long curly tail.
He loved the sand, the surf and the foam,
But he wished that he had a permanent home
In the sight of the harbor where tall-masted ships
Sailed in and out on adventurous trips.

Now Scuttle looked and looked for a house
For he wanted to be a home-owning mouse.
So he peeked in barrels, in kegs, in crates,
In boxes belonging to captains and mates.
But each time he hung up his sailor hat
He'd be chased from the place by a harbor rat!

Then Scuttle would hide by a barrel of fish
And in his mouse heart he would secretly wish
That he had the courage to sign on a ship—
A vessel off on a round-the-world trip.

But frankly, you see, if the truth were known,
Though Scuttle dreamed of a ship of his own,
He was really afraid of a boat with sails,
Of rolling breakers and gusty gales,
Of cargoes tossed on the churning seas;
For when he pictured such scenes as these
His tummy felt queer and his head spun around
And Scuttle was glad he was safe on the ground!

Now once when he thought he had found a place
Under a wharf, he came face to face
With a roving band of big harbor rats
In ragged trousers and battered hats.

**A**vast!" they cried. "Be off, you scum!
We rule this harbor, so don't you come
Snooping around if you value your life!"

**P**oor Scuttle shook as they held a knife
Right under his twittering, jittering nose.
He turned and ran till his small mouse toes
Were weary and sore. Then he came at last
To a huge sailing ship with a tall, tall mast.

The rats were close behind him now,
So he took one look at the vessel's prow,
Forgot his fears and dashed up the plank,
While the rats all snarled at him from the bank.

The captain shouted, "Ahoy! Heave ho!
Unfurl the sails! To sea we go!"

**S**cuttle scooted behind a crate.
Safely hidden, he knew he should wait
Till the ship was sailing with the tide.
Then stealthily Scuttle peeked out and spied
Some sailors at work on the rolling deck,
In gay colored suits with scarves at the neck.
Their captain was dressed in velvet and lace
And over one eye on his deep-scarred face
He wore a patch that made him look grim,
And his feathered hat had a turned-up brim.

**F**rom his hiding place the mouse could hear
What the captain said, for he stood quite near.

**A**t dawn we attack a ship," he said.
"The vessel sails not far ahead.
Ho! Ho! If only her captain and crew
Knew her fate as we pirates do!"

**A**ye, aye," laughed a wicked-looking mate,
"The Skull and Crossbones will seal their fate!"

**S**hiver my timbers!" poor Scuttle said.
"How I wish I were back on shore instead!
I've heard bloody tales of pirates at sea
Who rob and plunder—that's not for me!"

At dark the stowaway crept to the hold
Of the pirate ship. It was filled with gold!
There were chests of coins and kegs of wine
And casks with jewels of rich design.

They've already robbed a hundred men!"
Thought the dazzled mouse. "And they'll do it again!"

How right he was! At the break of day
Scuttle heard cannons booming away!
There were sounds of fighting above him on deck
And then came a crash—

And a terrible wreck!

**W**ater poured in through the leaky side.
"Oh, this is the end of my first ship ride!"
Cried Scuttle, trying his best to be brave
As he tossed and turned with each rolling wave.
"This is the end of my life at sea—
And it may even be the end of me!"

**S**cuttle thought fast. He must climb up high,
For the hold would be waterlogged by and by.
So, jumping from box to crate to bale,
He stayed quite dry—except for his tail.

As he perched on top of a wooden keg
Something thumped him hard on the leg.
A shower of coins like little gold moons
Came tumbling down—they were Spanish doubloons!

He held out his paws and what do you think?
He caught five gold pieces quick as a wink!
His pockets were small, so Scuttle the mouse
Tucked two more in the sleeve of his blouse.
He scooped up some smaller coins in his hat.
"I'll be rich!" he thought. "Just think of that!
But first I must get off this pirate ship,
For I'm sure it's made its very last trip."

Scuttle found a rope and began to pull.
But oh—it was hard—with his pockets so full!
Slowly he climbed up, paw over paw,
Till he reached the deck, and there he saw
Those bloody pirates with swords and knives
Yelling and fighting for their lives!

**I**n the midst of that battle he was so small
That nobody noticed the mouse at all.
Quickly Scuttle hunted around
Till over the railing he looked and found
The captain's hat with the turned-up brim—
A perfect boat for a mouse like him!

He hopped to the rail and jumped overboard
Carefully holding his golden hoard,
Wrapped in a pirate's bandana and tied,
To make it safe for the long sea ride.

Scuttle settled himself in the seaworthy hat
With its sail-like feather, long and fat.
The wind took him over the crest of the wave
Till suddenly Scuttle felt very brave.
He'd saved himself from a pirate ship!
And soon, with luck, his hat-boat trip
Would bring him back to his harbor once more
Where he could safely scuttle ashore.

His luck *was* good and by dark that night
A familiar harbor came into sight.
"I'm home!" he cried. "And after I land
I won't be chased by that ruffian band;
For now I have money to buy a small place
Of my own," he said, with a smile on his face.

**S**o Scuttle bought a new suit of clothes
And fine leather boots to cover his toes.
With a sword at his hip and a ring in his ear
He was Captain Scuttle, and when he'd appear
People would shout and clap their hands:
"That's the mouse who escaped from the pirate bands!"

Now the mayor was so impressed by the mouse
That he gave him a two-story, rat-proof house.

Scuttle bought a ship with the rest of his gold,
Spanking new from crow's nest to hold.
The *Jolly Roger* his ship was called,
But instead of pirate treasure it hauled
Cargoes of happy, vacationing mice—

Αnd he let the little ones sail half-price!

JEAN SOULE and her thirteen-year-old daughter, NANCY, have so far published three stories under their joint by-line.

Mrs. Soule is also the author of *Lenny's Twenty Pennies* and *Never Tease a Weasel*, both published by Parents' Magazine Press, as well as countless stories and poems for *Humpty Dumpty's Magazine* and other children's publications.

Nancy Soule is a student at Woodland Avenue Junior High School in Springfield, Pa., and she is interested in sports and art as well as writing. Besides the three stories she has co-authored with her mother, Nancy has had one poem of her own published in *Pet Fair* magazine.

BARBARA REMINGTON illustrated the paperback volumes of *The Lord of the Rings* by J. R. R. Tolkien and designed the popular "Middle Earth" posters based on the Tolkien trilogy. In addition to her work as a free-lance illustrator, she designs stuffed cloth animals and mobiles for store windows. She majored in art at the University of Minnesota and now lives in New York City with her husband, author Edward Preston.

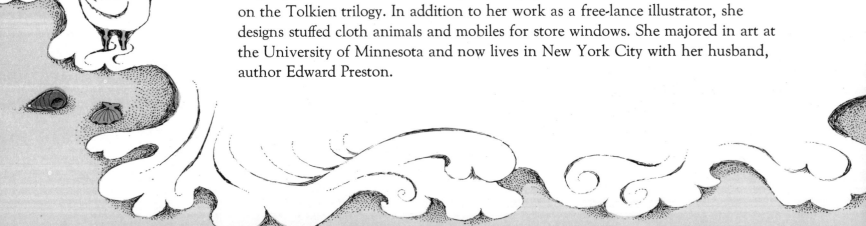